A Note to Parents and Caregivers:

Read-it! Readers are for children who are just starting on the amazing road to reading. These beautiful books support both the acquisition of reading skills and the love of books.

 The PURPLE LEVEL presents basic topics and objects using high frequency words and simple language patterns.

 The RED LEVEL presents familiar topics using common words and repeating sentence patterns.

 The BLUE LEVEL presents new ideas using a larger vocabulary and varied sentence structure.

 The YELLOW LEVEL presents more challenging ideas, a broad vocabulary, and wide variety in sentence structure.

 The GREEN LEVEL presents more complex ideas, an extended vocabulary range, and expanded language structures.

 The ORANGE LEVEL presents a wide range of ideas and concepts using challenging vocabulary and complex language structures.

When sharing a book with your child, read in short stretches, pausing often to talk about the pictures. Have your child turn the pages and point to the pictures and familiar words. And be sure to reread favorite stories or parts of stories.

There is no right or wrong way to share books with children. Find time to read with your child, and pass on the legacy of literacy.

Adria F. Klein, Ph.D.
Professor Emeritus
California State University
San Bernardino, California

Editor: Nick Healy
Designer: Abbey Fitzgerald
Page Production: Angela Kilmer
Art Director: Nathan Gassman
Associate Managing Editor: Christianne Jones
The illustrations in this book were created digitally.

Picture Window Books
5115 Excelsior Boulevard
Suite 232
Minneapolis, MN 55416
877-845-8392
www.picturewindowbooks.com

Printed in the United States of America.

Library of Congress Cataloging-in-Publication Data
Jenck, Heidi Shelton, 1960-
Gabe's grocery list / by Heidi Shelton Jenck ; illustrated by Zachary Trover.
p. cm. — (Read-it! readers)
Summary: Gabe and his little sister go shopping with their father and when
Gabe's shopping list differs from his father's, Gabe decides to take matter into
his own hands.
ISBN-13: 978-1-4048-3140-7 (library binding)
ISBN-10: 1-4048-3140-1 (library binding)
ISBN-13: 978-1-4048-1232-1 (paperback)
ISBN-10: 1-4048-1232-6 (paperback)
[1. Shopping—Fiction. 2. Fathers—Fiction. 3. Brothers and sisters—Fiction.]
I. Trover, Zachary, ill. II. Title.
PZ7.J4113Gab 2006
[E]—dc22   2006027293

s shopping day. Gabe made a list
e things.

Gabe's
Grocery List

by Heidi Shelton Jenck
illustrated by Zachary Trover

Special thanks to our advisers for their expertise:

Adria F. Klein, Ph.D.
Professor Emeritus, California State University
San Bernardino, California

Susan Kesselring, M.A.
Literacy Educator
Rosemount–Apple Valley–Eagan (Minnesota) School District

PICTURE WINDOW BOOKS
Minneapolis, Minnesota

Gabe loved writing lists more than anything in the world.

He wrote long l...
them on scraps ...
his walls.

Saturday wo...
of his favori...

He wanted lots of fruit.

My list:

1. oranges
2. lemons
3. grapes
4. apples
5. more fruit!

Dad made a grocery list, too. His list was full of vegetables for his favorite soup.

Gabe checked his list. "There are no vegetables on my list!" he told his little sister, Emma.

At the market, Dad went to find his vegetables.

Dad loved vegetables more than anything in the world.

"Lovely, lovely broccoli! Tra, la, la, la broccoli!" Dad sang like an opera star. He dropped broccoli into the shopping cart as he took a deep bow.

Broccoli was not on Gabe's list. He took it out of the cart and set it back on the shelf. He looked around for the apples and oranges.

"Beautiful, beautiful carrots!" said Dad, while he danced and tossed carrots into the cart.

"No, no, no! This is not on my list," Gabe said. Out went the carrots.

Gabe pointed to the apples, and Emma piled some into the cart.

Dad juggled onions and threw them into the cart.

"I did not put onions on my list," Gabe told his sister. Emma nodded, pinched her nose, and handed the onions to Mr. Pizak.

"Thanks!" he said. "Onions are on my list today."

"Yummy! This will be perfect for my soup," said Dad, hugging green, leafy spinach. Then he tossed it into the cart.

19

Gabe checked his list. "Nope, no leafy things on my list today," he told Mrs. Nagata. "Would you like this spinach?"

"Thank you!" she said. "I have spinach on my list today."

Each time Dad tossed vegetables into the cart, Gabe took them out. He and Emma put the vegetables back on the shelves or gave them to other shoppers.

They filled the cart with fruit. Emma found
fuzzy kiwifruit and bright red strawberries.
Gabe found ripe yellow bananas and plump
green grapes.

Dad tossed more vegetables into the cart. He crossed each one off of his list.

Gabe and Emma took the vegetables out.
They rounded up blueberries, lemons, and
a big watermelon.

Soon the cart was full of fruit. The cart was heavy and hard for Gabe to push.

Near the fish counter, Dad finally turned around. His eyes grew wide when he looked into the cart.

"Oh, no!" said Dad. "What happened to all of my vegetables?"

Gabe showed Dad his grocery list. Gabe said,
"Vegetables were not on my list today!"

My list:
1. oranges
2. lemons
3. grapes
4. apples
5. more fruit!

Dad smiled and said, "I guess we will have fruit salad tonight!"

More *Read-it!* Readers

Bright pictures and fun stories help you practice your reading skills. Look for more books at your level.

Benny and the Birthday Gift
The Best Lunch
The Boy Who Loved Trains
Car Shopping
Clinks the Robot
Firefly Summer
The Flying Fish
Loop, Swoop, and Pull!
Marvin, the Blue Pig
Paulette's Friend
Pony Party
Princess Bella's Birthday Cake
The Princesses' Lucky Day
Rudy Helps Out
The Sand Witch
Say "Cheese"!
The Snow Dance
The Ticket
Tuckerbean in the Kitchen

Looking for a specific title or level? A complete list of *Read-it!* Readers is available on our Web site:
www.picturewindowbooks.com